Mossycoat

Other brilliant stories to collect:

Mossycoat

Retold by
Philip Pullman

Illustrated by
Peter Bailey

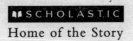
Home of the Story

Scholastic Children's Books,
Commonwealth House, 1–19 New Oxford Street,
London WC1A 1NU, UK
a division of Scholastic Ltd
London ~ New York ~ Toronto ~ Sydney ~ Auckland
Mexico City ~ New Delhi ~ Hong Kong

First published by Scholastic Ltd, 1998

ISBN 0 590 54392 X

Printed and bound by Mackays of Chatham

2 4 6 8 10 9 7 5 3 1

There once was a widow who lived in a cottage, and she had a daughter. The girl was lovely, though she didn't know it, and nor did she know what her mother was making, for that was a secret she hadn't been told yet. It was a waistcoat kind of a thing, made of the greenest moss all

sewn with gold thread that was finer than gossamer; and as for the stitches that held it together, no mortal ever stitched finer ones. A garment like that is a long time in making, you can be sure; the widow was young when she started, and many years older by the time it was nearly finished.

For it wasn't done, quite, when the story begins.

One day a hawker came to the door. He was a nuisance, this old man. He wasn't content to sell his ribbons and laces and needles and pins, but he had to make familiar remarks and wink and pinch the cheeks of girls too gentle to say no. He hadn't been seen for a while; some said he'd been locked up for his wickedness; at any rate, he was out and about again, and when he knocked at the door, it was the daughter who opened it.

"Well, hello!" he said. "You're a pretty one, ain't you?"

She didn't know how to answer

that. *He* wasn't pretty by any means: he was snaggle-toothed and red-nosed, with lank hair combed over his greasy bald pate, and he strutted like a cocky little dog.

"Here," he said, fumbling for her hand to pat it, "you're the prettiest thing I seen since . . . ooh, ever. You're prettier than them roses round the door, dang me if you ain't. Here, look at this. . ."

He plucked off a rose petal and held it against her cheek, and he ran his knobbly old fingers over them both.

"I can't tell the difference!" he said.

"You're as soft and smooth as —"

But she shook her head like a wild thing, as shy as a fawn.

"Ooh, I like you," he said. "You got a spark in you. You got some fizz and crackle. Now I don't believe in beating about the bush: I'm looking for a wife, and I believe you'd make a good 'un. How about it? Eh? Eh?"

He was nudging and winking and licking his lips, and his rheumy old eyes were glistening. The girl said, "Wait there."

She shut the door and ran in to her mother.

"Mum!" she said. "Mum! There's a horrible old hawker man at the door —"

"Oh, he's back, is he? What's he want?"

"He wants to marry me!"

"Well, do you want to marry him?"

"No, I don't!"

"All right," said her mother, "now you listen to me. You go and tell him that you'll marry him next week, as long as he brings you a dress. You understand? A white satin dress with gold sprigs on it, and it's got to fit you perfect."

"And will I have to marry him then?"

"Go and do as you're told."

So the girl went to the door and she said, "Well, I don't know. But if I do marry you, I need a proper wedding dress. You come back next week with a white satin dress all covered in gold sprigs this big, no *this* big, and we'll see. Oh, and it's got to fit me perfect."

"Hoo-hoo," chortled the hawker. "I'll be back! I'll be back! Giss a look at you, so I can judge your size."

He held out his thumb and squinted one eye and measured her up and

down, and off he went rubbing his hands.

Next week, there was a knock at the door, and the girl looked out of the window and ducked her head back quickly.

"Mum!" she said. "It's that blooming old hawker man, and he's got a parcel! What'm I going to do?"

"Go and answer the door, girl."

So she opened the door slowly.

"Oooh," said the hawker, "what a little peach! Yum-yum-yum! Here's your dress, girl, just like you wanted. Now when are you going to —"

"Hold on," said the girl, "I said it had to fit me perfect. I got to try it on first."

"Go on, then," said the hawker, and he gave her the parcel. "I'll wait here."

She took the parcel in to her mother.

"Mum, he's brought me the dress!" she said. "What am I going to do now?"

"Well, don't you want to try it on?"

They unwrapped the tissue paper and held up the dress. It was made of satin as white as snow, and the gold sprigs were all *this* big. And when she slipped it over her head and her mother fastened it up at the back, she found it fitted her like her own skin.

"Girl, you look beautiful," said her mother.

"But I can't marry him, he's horrible!"

"Well, tell him you need another dress. Ask for a silk one this time, the colour of all the birds of the air."

So she went back to the door. The

hawker was twitching and sniffing with impatience.

"Well?" he said. "Does it fit, then?"

"It's a bit tight under the arms," she said, "but I suppose it'll do to get married in. I can't go away for the honeymoon in a wedding dress, though, I need another dress for that. Make it silk, the colour of all the birds of the air."

"H'mm," he said. "And then. . . Mmm? Mmm? Eh?"

She just gave him a level kind of a look, and he made a whinnying sound and hurried away.

Next week, another knock.

"Mum, he's back again!"

"Open the door, then."

The hawker thrust the parcel into her hands, and tried to snatch a kiss while he was about it. She moved her face out of the way and shut the door.

"He's getting impatient, Mum! I can't put him off for ever!"

"Never mind that. Try the dress on, girl."

The silk dress fitted even better than the satin one had, and when she looked at herself in the mirror the girl felt dizzy to see the beautiful thing she was changing into. She wasn't sure if she liked it, but she knew she didn't like the hawker.

"What can I say to him?" she said in despair.

"Tell him you need some dancing shoes."

So she said to the hawker, "Well, I suppose the dresses are all right. But I expect there's to be dancing at the cel-ebrations, and unless you want to

dance with a bride in hob-nail boots,
you better get me some of them gold
patent-leather slippers with little
heels and diamond buckles. And if
they don't fit me perfect –"

"Right you are!" he said. "And
that's it, is it? Nothing else you
want?"

"No," she said, because she couldn't
think of anything else.

"Giss a look at your feet then."

He made a mark on a scrap of paper
to get the size.

"Next week, then!"

"All right. 'Bye."

Glumly she waited, and sure enough, next week there came his knock at the door.

"I got 'em! Diamond buckles and all! Now you got to marry me, girl, you can't keep me waiting any longer!"

"I got to try 'em on first," she said. "You probably made 'em too big. I got very little feet."

"Ooh, I guarantee they'll fit," he

said, winking and rubbing his hands.

She tried them on, and she didn't need a shoe-horn: they were neat and soft and light, neither too small nor too big, and they twinkled like fire-flies.

"Oh, Mum, what am I going to do now?" she wailed.

"Well now, girl," said her mother, "your mossy coat is all but ready. I should think another night's work'll see it done. So you go and tell the hawker to come back in the morning, about ten o'clock."

"What mossy coat?" said the girl.

"What are you talking about?"

"Shoo! Go and tell him, go on!"

So the girl opened the door once more. The hawker was licking his lips and rubbing his hands and panting and shifting from foot to foot.

"Well? Well? Well? Well? Well?" he said.

"The slippers are all right," she said. "The left one's a bit loose round the heel, but I suppose they'll do. You come back at ten in the morning, and I'll marry you."

"Ten in the morning? Why not now?"

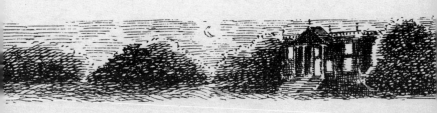

"Because I got to wash my hair, of course," she said. "Ten o'clock, and don't be late."

She shut the door before he could say another word. She could hear him snuffling and mumbling outside, but soon he gave up and left.

"Ten o'clock!" he called as he shut the garden gate. "Hoo! Hoo! Hoo!"

"Mum —" the girl began, but her mother shook her head.

"Don't you say a word, because I'm going to be busy all night. Fetch that old suitcase off the top of the wardrobe and pack them dresses in it,

and the slippers too, wrap 'em all in tissue paper, go on. Then bring me a cup of tea."

All night long the woman sewed. She worked till three whole candles had burned down and the daylight had come again, and just as the cock was crowing she snapped off the last gold thread with her aching fingers.

She stretched and yawned and woke

the girl.

"Now you better get up," she said, "because if you lie there snoring and steaming all morning you're going to find yourself a-married to that old hawker whether you want to be or not. Get out of bed and wash yourself and then come down to the parlour. And bring the suitcase."

A few minutes later the girl, clean and wide awake and fearful, lugged the suitcase downstairs.

"What's that?" she said. "Is that the mossy coat?"

Her mother held it up against her.

It was as green as a spring morning, as fresh and soft as a breeze out of the west. All the mosses her mother had gathered from pond and meadow and millstream over eighteen years were bright and living yet: she'd plaited and woven them so cunningly that all the tiny moss-leaves were still alive. And under and over and in between them all lay a shimmer of gold from those gossamer threads stitched with stitches too small to see. The mossy coat was so light and fine you could fold it all into a thimble, and yet so strong you couldn't tear it with your teeth.

And the best part was, it was magic. The daughter was to wear it under her other clothes when she wanted to make a wish, and whatever she wished for would come true.

"Oh, mother," the girl breathed, slipping her arms into it and hugging it close to her breast.

"Yes," said her mother, "this is for you, my dear. From now on, you're going to be called Mossycoat. That's your name in the future. I been a-stitching and a-gathering since you were born, and now you're ready for it, and it's time for you to leave and

find your way in the world, my dear. You must go and seek your fortune, and a fine fortune it'll be. Take up the suitcase, and close your eyes, and wish you were a hundred miles away."

"But what about him?"

"You leave him to me," said her mother. "Go on! Go!"

So Mossycoat took the suitcase in her right hand, and clenched her left hand firmly around the front of the mossy coat, and closed her eyes and wished. And as soon as the wish was formed in her mind, whoosh! Up she swept into the air, like a leaf in a

storm, but she clung to the suitcase as tight as a limpet, and she clutched the mossy coat firm around her front.

Where she flew she couldn't tell, for she kept her eyes well shut; but presently all the whooshing died away, and then the soles of her feet touched ground and all her weight came back to her, and she tottered a step or two and opened her eyes.

And there she was, in a different part of the country altogether. To her left was a river with green meadows beyond it, and to her right there were orchards and farmyards all neat and

prosperous, and ahead of her was a
hill, and on the top of the hill was a
fine brick house with rose-beds in
front and tulips standing to attention
like soldiers along the gravel drive.

"Well," said Mossycoat to herself, "I
can't stand here gaping all day."

So first she took off her mossy coat
and folded it away safe in the suitcase,
and then she climbed the hill in the

warm sunshine with the birds singing and the breeze lifting the scent out of the apple-blossom, and she knocked on the door of the big house.

"Excuse me for knocking," she said to the lady of the house, "but I've just arrived in this land, and I need a job."

The lady was a kind sort of a person, and shrewd, and she liked the look of this young girl with her suit-case; so she said, "And what can you do, my dear? Can you sew, or polish, or what?"

"I can cook a bit," said Mossycoat. "There's some says I'm quite a good

cook, or I will be with practice."

"Well," said the lady, "if we needed a cook we'd try you out; but I tell you what," she said, "I'll give you a job in the kitchen and see how you get on."

"Thank you, ma'am," said Mossycoat, and she followed the lady into the house.

And such a house it was: a grand hall with a staircase all hung with paintings, and a drawing-room with gilded furniture and Chinese carpets, and a dining-room with a mahogany table so shiny that the silver candelabra seemed to be floating

on dark water. The lady took Mossycoat up to a little bedroom in the attic and showed her where she could sleep and put her suitcase, and then took her down to the kitchen.

On the way through the hall there was a commotion, as a young man came in dressed for hunting, with half a dozen big floppy dogs all leaping up and licking him. Mossycoat took one glance at him, and then she kept her eyes modestly downwards and stood as meek as a nun.

"Who's this, mother?" said the young man.

"She's our new kitchen maid," said the lady. "Come this way, my dear, and I'll show you where you'll be working."

Mossycoat followed her into the kitchen. All the cooks and the under-cooks and the bottle-washers and the pantry-maids and the scullery-maids stopped what they were doing and looked at Mossycoat, and she just kept quiet and looked down. The lady explained what Mossycoat's duties would be, and then she left the kitchen.

As soon as she'd gone, the servants started.

"Look at her! Lady Muck!"

"Who does she think she is?"

"Too grand for the likes of us — little snob!"

"Sucking up to madam! There's no sucking up in the kitchen — no airs and graces in here!"

The head cook said: "What's your name, then?"

"Mossycoat," she said.

"Mossycoat? Bossyboots, more like. You're one of the workers now. None of your high-and-mighty ways down here — we'll knock that out of you quick enough, see if we don't."

They were a very low kind of people in that kitchen. They had just enough sense to know what was better than they were, and just enough energy to hate it.

So Mossycoat set to work, and they gave her the dirtiest jobs: cleaning the sooty grease off the spits, scrubbing the scullery floor, scraping the mud

off the potatoes. And they never stopped calling her names and mocking her, although she just kept herself quiet and modest and gave them no reason to. And every so often, when her back was turned, some oaf would take the skimmer, all greasy from the soup, and knock her on the head with it; and she never once complained or tried to hit back. What with all the work and the harsh treatment, her clothes were soon covered in grease and dirt, and her face and hair and fingernails were sadly grubby.

Now a little while later, it was announced that there were going to be three days of merry-making in a great house nearby. There was to be music, and dancing, and feasting, and fireworks, and invitations were sent out to all the houses in the district. Of course the master and mistress were invited, and the young master too, and it was the talk of the kitchen.

"I wish I could go – I'm as good as

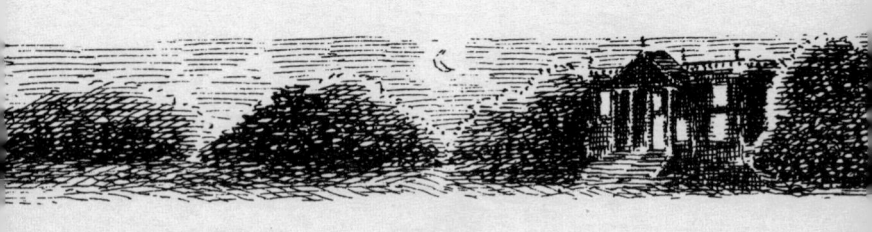

they are any day of the week!"

"All them lovely dresses. . ."

"All them handsome young men! Eh?"

Mossycoat said nothing. But all this time, the mistress of the house had been watching her, and she noticed what the servants didn't: she saw how clever and modest little Mossycoat was, and how pretty she was too, under the grime.

So she sent for her and said, "Now, Mossycoat, how would you like a treat? How would you like to come to the ball with us, as our guest?"

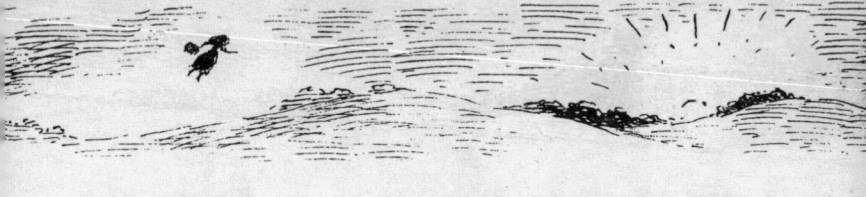

"Well, ma'am," said Mossycoat, "that's very kind of you, but I think I'd better not, on account of being so grubby. I'd make your carriage all greasy if I sat in it. And I wouldn't know how to behave at a grand affair like that, and I'd let you down. Thank you kindly, but you'd be better off not taking me."

"Well, are you sure?" said the lady, but Mossycoat wouldn't be budged.

When she went back to the kitchen, the servants were all agog to know why she'd been sent for.

"Did she give you notice?"

"Are they getting rid of you?"

"What did she say?"

Mossycoat said, "The mistress asked me to the ball, and I said no."

"You blooming liar!"

"Did you hear that?"

"She says they asked her to the ball! Ruddy nerve!"

And out came the skimmer, and poor Mossycoat's head rang.

The first night of the festivities were such a success that the lady of the house sent for Mossycoat again.

"Mossycoat, my dear, are you sure you wouldn't like to come? I know you'd enjoy it! And the master would like you to join us, and the young master too. There's going to be fireworks tonight!"

"Thank you kindly, ma'am, but I think I'd better not," said Mossycoat.

But that evening, when the servants were all sitting round idly in the kitchen smoking or playing cards or gossiping, Mossycoat went to her room. First she washed herself from head to foot, and cleaned all the soot and grime and dirt off her skin and out of her hair. Then she slipped the mossy coat on and went down to the kitchen. She went round from one servant to the next, touching each of them and wishing, and as she touched them they fell asleep, their great greasy heads lolling down on the table or back open-mouthed in their chairs.

When they were all fast asleep and snoring, she went up and put on her white satin dress with the gold sprigs, and the golden slippers, and she wished herself at the festivities.

Up she flew, through the warm night air, and down she was set outside the ballroom. The band was playing a waltz, and the chandeliers were glowing, and the movement of the ladies and gentlemen on the dancefloor was like swans on a lake.

Well, no sooner had Mossycoat arrived than the young master saw her. He didn't recognize her, but he said to his mother: "Look at that girl in the white dress, mother! Isn't she beautiful? Where does she come from, I wonder?"

"If you go and ask her to dance, you might find out," his mother said.

So he came up to her and asked for the next dance. She looked him full in the eyes and said, "Thank you, sir, but I'd rather not dance just yet."

And she wouldn't dance with him, nor with anyone else, and he had to be content with that. Nor would she tell him her name, nor where she came from, and for all he begged to know,

she just laughed and teased and said,
"That's my secret."

The only comfort he had was that
she wouldn't talk to anyone else
either, though she was gracious and
polite and so lovely to look at that all
the young men in the place clustered
round to flirt.

Finally the young master went to
his mother and said, "Mother, if I
don't find out who she is I'll go mad
with despair, but she won't tell me.
Can you ask her for me?"

The lady sat down with Mossycoat
on the terrace, and they sipped their

wine and chatted. But the lady got no more out of her than her son; all the strange girl would tell her was that she came from a place where they hit her on the head with a skimmer.

"What sort of a place is that?" said the lady in surprise.

"Oh, I shouldn't think I'll be there long," was all Mossycoat said in reply.

Then came the last dance, and the young master tried once more. "Please dance with me!" he said. "I'm longing to dance, and there's no one else I want to dance with but you."

"Well," said Mossycoat, "just this

once, then."

And she held out her hand, and he led her to the dance floor. She was as light in his arms as a bird of the air, he'd never found dancing so easy and joyful; but it didn't last, for no sooner had they danced down to the end of the ballroom than she slipped out of his grasp and away through the door.

"No! Wait! Come back!" he cried, and he ran out after her, but there was nothing there in the dark, nothing at all, only the warm breeze and the stars and his beating heart.

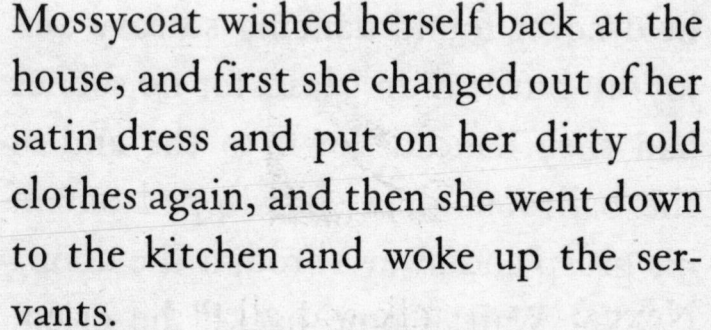

Mossycoat wished herself back at the house, and first she changed out of her satin dress and put on her dirty old clothes again, and then she went down to the kitchen and woke up the servants.

"Have we been asleep all this time?" said the pastrycook.

"Oh! You won't tell, will you, Mossycoat?" said the scullery-maid.

"If you keep us out of trouble, I'll

let you have my old dress," said the
housekeeper.

"I won't say a word," said Mossycoat, and nor did she.

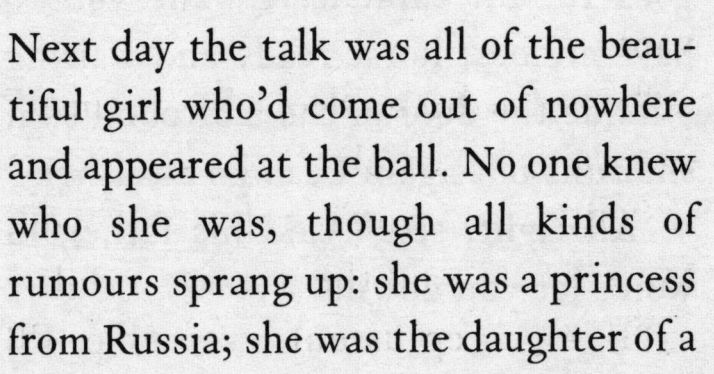

Next day the talk was all of the beautiful girl who'd come out of nowhere
and appeared at the ball. No one knew
who she was, though all kinds of
rumours sprang up: she was a princess
from Russia; she was the daughter of a

millionaire; she wasn't a mortal at all, she was a fairy. And everyone was buzzing to see whether she'd turn up for the last night of the festivities.

As for the young master, he was desperate.

"Father," he said, "if I don't find out who that girl is and where she goes to, I'll explode. I want you to have my best horse ready and waiting outside the door of the ballroom, so if she runs out again I can go after her."

"All right, son," said his father, "I won't let you down."

That evening Mossycoat put the servants to sleep again, and this time she put on her silk dress the colour of all the birds of the air. And when she arrived at the ball this time, there was the young master at once, at the head of all the other young men desperate to dance with her; for word had got around, and there wasn't anyone within fifty miles who hadn't heard of this mysterious girl who appeared out of

nowhere and disappeared again.

Mossycoat answered no questions
except with a smile, and she wouldn't
dance with anyone – except, once
again, with the young master.

He was as proud and happy as a
king; down the ballroom they danced,
and up again to the orchestra, and
never had such a handsome couple
been seen in anyone's memory. Then
with a twirl in the music, the two of
them turned and danced to the door –

And the young master must have
loosened his grip in the heat of the
moment, for she was out of his arms

and away.

And straight he ran after her into the dark, and there was his horse with the groom at the reins —

"Oh, where did she go? Which way? Did you see her?"

No sign! Not a glimpse! She was vanished and gone. The horse shook his head and jingled his bridle, and stamped a hoof on the stones of the terrace; and the young master ran this way and that, gazing into the dark, calling, imploring the girl with no name to come back, for he loved her. . .

Nothing. Silence. Darkness.

The heartless music played on in the ballroom, and he heard none of it. Then as he turned in despair, he saw something catching the light, something down on the gravel below the windows, a little golden twinkle.

Her slipper! She'd dropped a slipper as she vanished! He clutched it to his heart. It was all that was left of that beautiful stranger, all that he had to take home from the ball.

Well, next day you never heard such a to-do.

It was the talk of every house in the

county – the girl who'd won everyone's heart with her grace and her beauty, the young man she chose from all of the others to be her dancing-partner; and how she was nowhere to be found, and how he was lying ill in bed with a mysterious fever.

Mossycoat heard the rumours in the kitchen, with all the other servants.

"He's ill? The young master?"

"Groaning and sickening something terrible. . ."

"What's wrong with him?"

"They're in fear for his life!"

The doctor was sent for. He arrived

in his carriage as soon as he could, and went straight up to the wild-eyed young patient. He tested his temperature and timed his pulse; he took his stethoscope out of his top hat and listened to the thumping of the young man's heart; he tapped his chest and peered into his eyes, and then he heard a broken whisper. The great physician stooped to listen closer, and then he saw what the young man clutched so tight in his hand.

He stood up straight and made his diagnosis.

"This is no fever," he said solemnly.

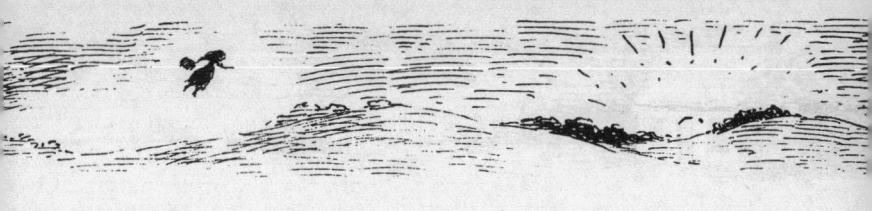

"Nor is it an infection, nor a case of poisoning, nor a plague or a pox or a murrain. This is an affliction of the heart."

"Oh no!" said the lady of the house, and she stroked the damp hair off her son's pallid brow.

"The patient is in love," the doctor explained. "That's the long and the short of it, and if he doesn't find the object of his affection, his heart will give way altogether. You must find the girl who fits this slipper – " and he held up the young man's trembling hand, still clutching the golden slipper

– "or else, send for the sexton to dig the patient's grave. My fee is ten guineas. Good morning."

So that was the state of things. Word went out at once all over the countryside, and girls by the hundred came flocking to try the slipper, for it was announced that the young man was heir to a splendid fortune as well as being ardent and handsome. A line of

girls led up the stairs, out through the hall, along the drive, and halfway down the hill, and still more of them came from every direction.

And you never saw such feet: long knobbly ones, short fat ones, graceful ones but just too big, ones covered in corns and bunions, flat ones, warty ones, pretty ones and tender ones; but not a single one that fitted the slipper.

Eventually, when the last girl tugged her stocking up with a sigh and trudged off down the hill, the lady of the house said, "We've tried everything else, my dear; we shall have to

ask the servants."

You can imagine the glee at that. Every female servant in the house crowded and jostled to shove her foot in the golden slipper, but of course none of them could do it, not even by holding their breath and squeezing.

The lady said, "Is that everyone? I didn't see Mossycoat."

"Oh, her," said someone, but they had to fetch her.

She came up the stairs all quiet and modest. Her hair was dusty, there was a smudge of soot on her cheek, and anything less like the girl of the night

before would be hard to find; but the lady saw through her, and she felt a lift in her heart as Mossycoat slipped off her grimy shoe and took up the slipper.

And it fitted.

The young master gave a cry of joy, but Mossycoat held up her hand.

"No," she said, "wait. I'm not ready yet."

She ran up to her bedroom and washed and put on the white satin dress, and the other slipper, and then came down to the young master's room, where all the family was waiting

to welcome her. The young master ran to her and opened his arms, but again she said:

"Wait. I've changed my mind. I'm going to put my other dress on."

So she went up and changed, and then she came down once more, and this time she didn't say, "Wait."

Well, he nearly ate her.

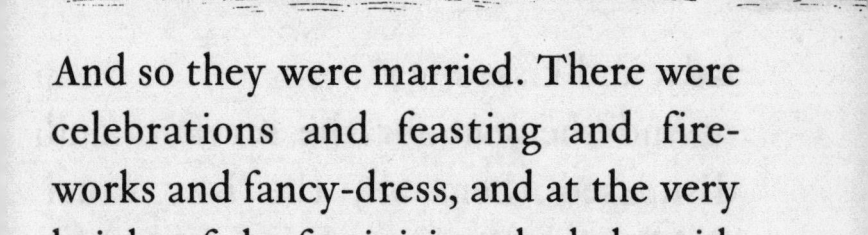

And so they were married. There were celebrations and feasting and fireworks and fancy-dress, and at the very height of the festivities, the lady said, "Now tell me, Mossycoat dear, when we talked at the ball you told me you came from a place where they hit you on the head with a skimmer. Was that true?"

"Perfectly true," said Mossycoat.

"And where was that place?"

"Well, it was in your kitchen," said Mossycoat. "And I said I didn't think I'd be there for long."

"That was true enough," said the

lady, and kissed her.

And she sent for the servants and dismissed them all, the lazy cruel slubberdegullions, and set about hiring a better lot of servants altogether.

As for Mossycoat and her husband, they had a basket of children, and they're living there now in the house on the hill, as far as I know.